Great Explorers

ZEBULON PIKE

Stephen Krensky

A Crabtree Crown Book

Crabtree Publishing
crabtreebooks.com

School-to-Home Support for Caregivers and Teachers

This appealing book is designed to teach students about core subject areas. Students will build upon what they already know about the subject, and engage in topics that they want to learn more about. Here are a few guiding questions to help readers build their comprehensions skills. Possible answers appear here in red.

Before Reading:

What do I know about this topic?
- *I know that Zebulon Pike was an American explorer that led an expedition.*
- *I know that the tallest mountain peak Pike found was later named Pike's Peak.*

What do I want to learn about this topic?
- *I want to learn more about the maps and notes that Pike drew and wrote.*
- *I want to learn more about the Indigenous peoples Pike and his men encountered.*

During Reading:

I'm curious to know...
- *I'm curious to know if Pike made contact with the Comanche tribe.*
- *I'm curious to know if any of Pike's companions started a mutiny when they had to camp in snowy conditions.*

How is this like something I already know?
- *I know that many Native American tribes were protective of their hunting grounds.*
- *I know that Zebulon Pike was a great leader.*

After Reading:

What was the author trying to teach me?
- *I think the author was trying to teach me about the accomplishments of Zebulon Pike in his short life.*
- *I think the author was trying to teach me about the effects of the Louisiana Purchase.*

How did the photographs and captions help me understand more?
- *The maps helped me understand the areas explored by Pike.*
- *The picture of the buffalo was a reminder to me of how many buffalo roamed America before they were hunted by settlers for their hides and meat.*

Table of Contents

Chapter 1:
Expeditions on the Move

Zebulon Pike looked around at the roughly two dozen people gathered nearby. The scene was very **familiar**. Pike was about to be on the move. His saddlebags were packed. His horses were fed. His orders were securely tucked away. Pike was going to set out from Missouri, leading a small group on an important **mission**. He knew many of them well from earlier experiences. They were, as he later wrote, "perfectly capable of getting the job done," but also a set of "rascals."

The 1806 expedition had several goals. First, Pike was tasked to explore and report on the land in the south and west of the Louisiana Purchase. Three years prior, the U.S. government had purchased the **territory** of Louisiana—828 square miles (2,140,000 sq. km.)—from France. Most of this land was **inhabited** by Native American tribes. So Pike was also asked to make contact with some of these tribes, including the Comanche. Lastly, Pike was meant to **escort** about 50 Osage people, who had been held captive, back to their home.

Native Americans

keelboat

A year earlier, in 1805, Pike had undertaken a different assignment heading north from St Louis. He and 20 soldiers traveled north on a 70-foot (21-m) keelboat. The keelboat had runways on each side where the soldiers could walk along and push the boat using long poles. All together, the trip covered 2000 miles (3,219 km).

Pike's job had been to find the **headwaters** of the Mississippi, to select some sites for future military posts, and to establish relationships with any Native American tribes he met.

Pike had also carried a message for any British fur traders he came upon. In the future, they would no longer be welcome to hunt at will on American land. And what if the fur traders objected to this news? Pike was hoping for peaceful exchanges, but, if necessary, he was prepared to convince the traders at the point of a rifle barrel.

American land

Neither of these trips had come as a surprise. After the Louisiana Purchase in 1803, there was much to discover about the new U.S. territory. It stretched from the Mississippi River in the east, to the Rocky Mountains in the west, and north to present-day Canada. President Thomas Jefferson had paid 15 million dollars at a time when the average worker earned about a dollar a day. For eighteen dollars per square mile, the sale was a real bargain. And it included the bustling port of New Orleans, which sat at the juncture of the Mississippi River and the Gulf of Mexico.

Such a vast territory almost doubled the size of the United States in a single stroke. But what did it look like up close? What was the best way to get from one end to the other? Almost no one knew anything about its rivers, mountains, or valleys—except for **Indigenous** peoples who had lived in the area for many years. Those running the U.S. were eager to gain this knowledge, too.

No single expedition could give Jefferson and his advisors a complete picture of what they had bought. Several other trips of discovery were already in the works, and more were planned for the near future.

Louisiana Purchase

Chapter 2: Onward to Colorado

Meanwhile, the Pike Expedition, as it came to be known, set out on July 15, 1806. As Pike wrote: "Our party consisted of two lieutenants, one **surgeon**, one sergeant, two corporals, 16 privates, and one interpreter. We had also under our charge chiefs of the Osage and Pawnees, who, with a number of women and children, had been to Washington."

Pike's first task was to ensure the Osage tribe members made it back to their communities. Once he did that, he continued on his way. Pike paid close attention to his surroundings as he traveled. One of his jobs was to identify natural resources such as forests, minerals, or good farmland.

As a seasoned explorer, Pike was right at home out west. He was used to hunting, scouting, and keeping an eye out for threats such as wolves, bears, and poisonous snakes.

Osage chief

However, Pike hadn't started out that way. He was born near Lamberton, New Jersey in 1779. Lamberton was not a bustling city, but it was hardly the **frontier**. At the time, the American Revolution was still raging. Pike's father, Zebulon Pike Sr., was serving in the Continental Army.

Members of the Continental Army

Cincinnati 1800

CINCINNATI-1800.

Later, after peace was declared, the Pikes moved to the Northwest Territory, south of the Great Lakes. There, Zebulon Pike Sr. held various military posts.

Young Pike grew up moving from place to place before settling for a few years in the new town of Cincinnati. When he was 15, Pike became a **cadet** under his father's command and learned how to be a soldier. In 1796, at the age of 17, he was part of a group that kept an eye on some French soldiers who were mapping the borders of their land with the new United States.

As Pike passed through Kansas, the vast open spaces he was crossing were almost overwhelming. Amidst this open landscape, Pike could take note of the western horizon when he started out at dawn, travel all day, and see an unchanged horizon at dusk.

Along the way, Pike noticed the huge herds of buffalo that roamed over the plains. "The face of the prairie was covered with them, on each side of the river," he wrote in his journal. "Their number **exceeded** imagination." From a hilltop, he saw buffalo, elk, deer, antelope, and panthers all at the same time.

Chapter 3:
Scaling a Summit

Then, Pike moved on to Colorado. Almost everywhere, he saw clear signs, such as old footprints or deserted campfires, that both Native Americans and Spanish soldiers were in the area. But they mostly avoided any contact.

On November 15, Zeb first saw the mountain that he called the "Grand Peak." At 14,000 feet (4,267 m) high, it was the tallest mountain they had discovered. Later, it would bear Pike's name.

Pike assumed that the view from the summit would be well worth a look. He took three men with him to attempt the climb while the rest stayed in the base camp they built on the site of the future town of Pueblo.

Unfortunately, Pike and his men weren't properly dressed for the bitter cold that came early to the higher elevations. As the snow continued to fall, their progress was slow and painful. When the fallen snow reached up to their waists, every foot forward became a struggle.

At the summit, they found the view as spectacular as they had hoped. Unfortunately, it was not the view from the "Grand Peak" they had seen earlier from a distance. The men accidentally climbed a smaller peak nearby. Another 14 years would pass before Edwin James became the first person credited with scaling the "Grand Peak."

The men returned to their base camp, but by now it was clear that no further summits would be reached. The weather was just too cold. Many of their companions were suffering. Their cheeks and noses were frozen. They had **frostbite** on their feet, making it difficult to walk.

The situation was grim, as Pike described it in his journal. They were, he noted, "800 miles [1,287 km] from the frontiers of our country, in the most **inclement** season of the year—not one person clothed for the winter—many without blankets, having been obliged to cut them up for socks, etc., and now lying down at night on the snow or wet ground, one side burning whilst the other was pierced with the cold wind."

Chapter 4: A Wrong Turn

Clearly, the group was in great danger. If the expedition stayed where it was, no one would survive. But not everyone was fit to travel. So, while promising to return for the injured men later, Pike led the remaining group through a promising mountain pass only to halt in the face

of ever deepening snow. As he wrote in his journal, "for the first time in the voyage [I] found myself discouraged."

Turning south, they came to what they thought was the Red River. There, they built a **stockade** with heavy logs and a defensive ditch. They sent a few men back to retrieve the injured travelers and planned to recover there for most of the winter.

In fact, though, this river was the Rio Grande. The expedition had wandered out of the Louisiana Purchase and into Spanish

territory. So when a troop of Spanish soldiers came upon them a few weeks later, in February 1807, they were taken prisoner. First, they were brought to the town of Santa Fe for questioning. Then, they were moved 500 miles (805 km) further south to the territorial capital of Chihuahua in Mexico.

Pike being led by the Spanish in Santa Fe

The Spanish who controlled Mexico had never been happy about the Louisiana Purchase. They had even controlled the vast area of land for few decades, before control went back to France who then sold it to the United States. They were even more unhappy to find American soldiers wandering over the border into their territory.

Pike tried to explain that they meant the Spanish no harm. Their presence was simply a mistake. But the Spanish remained cautious. Still, Pike and his companions were treated politely. They were not considered prisoners, exactly, but they were also not permitted to leave. It took several months of **negotiations** with American authorities before the expedition was escorted to the border of Louisiana and allowed to go home. When he got back, Pike had been gone 353 days, and traveled a total of 3,664 miles (5,897 km).

Having survived two dangerous journeys out west, Pike returned to army life. He was posted to different positions in the Midwest and was promoted several times for his efforts. On November 7, 1811, he took part in the Battle of Tippecanoe near Lafayette, Indiana led by then Governor (and later President) William Henry Harrison.

General Pike

Battle of Tippecanoe

However, Pike's luck ran out two years later while fighting in the War of 1812. While commanding an advance guard of soldiers near what was later Toronto, Canada, Pike was killed when a stockpile of ammunition exploded nearby. He was 34 years old.

An 1839 engraving shows the death of American brigadier general Zebulon Pike at the Battle of York.

Chapter 5:
The Final Campaign

Zeb's life may have been cut short, but his accomplishments lived on. He had written a detailed report of his travels for the government, and in 1810, published a book including his journal and letters. Many later travelers used his maps and descriptions to guide their footsteps. In this way, Zebulon Pike remained a presence on the American frontier for many years to come.

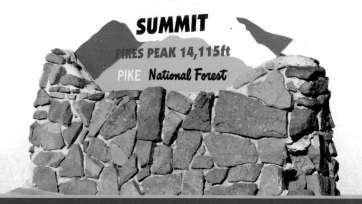

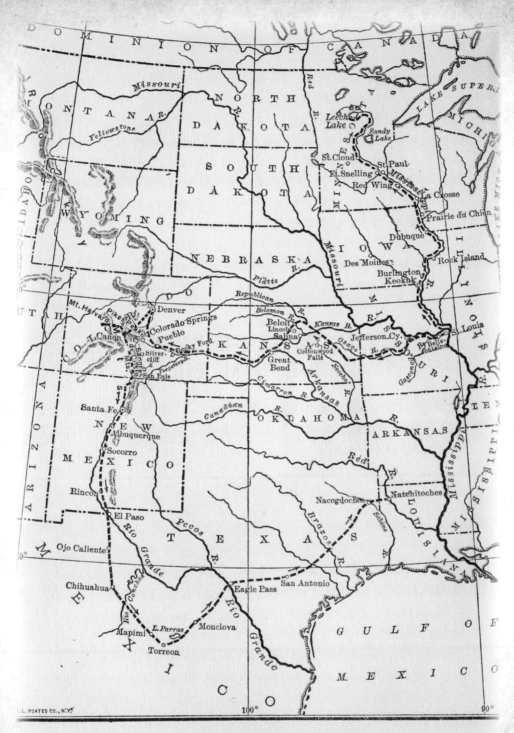

MAP OF PIKE'S EXPLORATIONS
The dotted lines show the routes followed on the several expeditions

Glossary

cadet: A military student who is being trained to be a soldier

escort: To accompany and keep safe

exceeded: Going beyond what is expected

Indigenous: Describes the first inhabitants of a place

inhabited: Lived in

familiar: Well known from repeated contact

frontier: A wilderness or largely uninhabited area of land

frostbite: A medical condition where the skin has been damaged, often permanently, from extreme cold

headwaters: The source of a river

inclement: Of weather, severe or harsh

mission: An important assignment

negotiations: Discussions meant to resolve disputes or create agreements

stockade: A crude fort often built with logs

surgeon: A doctor who specializes in performing surgeries, or treating injuries by operating on the body

territory: An area of land controlled by a leader, group, or country

Index

Comprehension Questions

How many acres were in the Louisiana Purchase?

How tall is the "Grand Peak," which was later named after Zebulon Pike?

What were the goals of Pike's expedition?

About the Author

Stephen Krensky is the award-winning author of more than 150 fiction and nonfiction books for children. He and his wife Joan live in Lexington, Massachusetts, and he happily spends as much time as possible with his grown children and not-so-grown grandchildren.

Written by: Stephen Krensky
Designed by: Rhea Wallace
Series Development: James Earley
Proofreader: Janine Deschenes
Educational Consultant: Marie Lemke M.Ed.
Print Coordinator: Katherine Berti

Photo credits: Fulton H Powers: cover background; Morphart Creation: cover; Morphart Creation: p. 1; daniilphotos: p. 4; LOC: p. 5; LOC: p. 6; LOC: p. 7; LOC: p. 9; Ondrej Prosicky: p. 11; LOC: p. 11; LOC: p. 12; LOC: p. 13; Tami Freed: p. 14; Nosyrevy: p. 16; Sarah Fields Photography: p. 17; D. Scott Larson: p. 18; kasakphoto: p. 21; British Library's collections: p. 22; LOC: p. 24; LOC: p. 24; LOC: p. 26; LOC: p. 26; LOC: p. 27; MostDefinitely: p. 28; public domain: p. 28; LOC: p. 29;

Crabtree Publishing

crabtreebooks.com   800-387-7650

Printed in the U.S.A./012023/CG20220815

Published in Canada
Crabtree Publishing
616 Welland Ave.
St. Catharines, Ontario
L2M 5V6

Published in the United States
Crabtree Publishing
347 Fifth Ave
Suite 1402-145
New York, NY 10016

Library and Archives Canada Cataloguing in Publication
Available at Library and Archives Canada

Library of Congress Cataloging-in-Publication Data
Available at the Library of Congress

Hardcover: 978-1-0398-0012-0
Paperback: 978-1-0398-0071-7
Ebook (pdf): 978-1-0398-0190-5
Epub: 978-1-0398-0130-1